THRONE OF KAALAGHAT

A JOURNEY OF BRUTALITY...

BY

PRASHANT MOHA..

Detailed Information about the Book

Authored By: PRASHANT MOHAN

Editing and Proofread by: P. Verma

Publication Format: Amazon Kindle E-Book format, paperback

Edition No: First Edition

Publication From: Mumbai, India

Publication Year: 2022

Version: International

E-Mail address: pmvermabbk@gmail.com

Kaalan; the king of the Kaalaghat jungle was moving with pack of wolves towards the graveyard for the funeral of his wife; Paatali. His moves were languished and eyes teary. The graveyard was in the north of the Kaalaghat jungle. Lukata and her hyena sisters; Putani and Mandha were noticing everything from the horrible rocks; in the graveyard's north.

The graveyard was sandwiched between the Kaalaghat jungle and Rock-field. About two-hundred hyenas were living in Rock-field.

"We will never be gifted again with such a prolific opportunity to dethrone wolves from the Kaalaghat throne." Lukata looked at her sisters and said.

"You are right, Lukata. The entire pack of wolves is experiencing the pain of the death of its queen, and this is the right time to press their nerves and dethrone them from Kaalaghat throne." Putani said in excitement.

"Kaalan is the king of the Kaalaghat jungle for namesake. The diplomatic brain behind the wolves ruling was of Paatali." whispered Lukata.

"But it seems Kaalan's body is made of steel. He can kill five-six hyenas alone simultaneously." Mandha said.

"Stop praising the enemy. Sometime, I get bemused, whether you are a wolf or a hyena….. But you are right. His stealth body is the reason that we could never try for the Kaalaghat throne." Lukata looked at Mandha and exclaimed.

"Sooner we will send Kaalan to meet his wife, and Kaalaghat throne would be of hyenas." Putani said and grinned. Lukata and Mandha smiled after listening to Putani.

"I think we should also go to the funeral of Paatali." Mandha said in excitement.

"Because of unexpected God gifted glee- I think your brain stopped operating properly." Lukata stared at Mandha in anger, and scolded. Mandha replied nothing, but gave a submissive look.

"But how will we kill Kaalan?"

"Don't get overexcited. Enjoy the death of Paatali for now. Later, we will chalk out the plan of death for the Kaalaghat bastard." Lukata replied.

Hyenas had ruined all the natural beauty of Rock-field. Very fewer trees and bushes were available over there. Only horrible rocks were available in a plethora, and hyenas were eyeing the Kaalaghat jungle to make it the ground for their game of blood.

After-cremating the dead body of Paatali, Kaalan and the entire pack of wolves were returning from the graveyard. All the faces were radiating optimum mourn- the reason for glee on hyenas faces. As the wolves entered inside the Kaalaghat jungle, Lukata and other hyenas also returned to their place inside Rock-field.

Time was passing and all the wolves were sitting in tears. Colour of the Sun was getting reddish and size bigger, when Kaalan started feeling some uneasiness. He was looking like a defeated and captured king in a war- waiting for his death. Grief of the death of Paatali had suppressed his zeal completely towards the welfare of the Kaalaghat jungle and its animals. Time was moving with the extra propeller, and the condition of the king was deteriorating unexpectedly faster.

Noticing the condition of the king alarming, his sons; Suggha and Bhallad called Dr. Furti; doctor of wolves, to monitor the health of the king. Dr. Furti reached there hurriedly, and started monitoring king Kaalan's health in a haste. But within no time king's neck started lolling and his body got loosen in toto. Dr. Furti was leaving no stone unturned to get the king's breaths back, but his all efforts were going in vain. Watching tears in Dr. Furti's eyes, Suggha and Bhallad broke into tears.

After checking thoroughly, Dr. Furti declared the sad demise of the king Kaalan, with teary eyes. Listening to him, the wave of the mourn surged through the jungle animals. But, the news of king's sudden death mesmerized hyenas in the rock-field.

"Wow! this is the most idyllic day in our lives. Two most powerful entities of the rivals have left the ground within a day. Now, nobody can stop us from ruling Kaalaghat as per our will." Lukata said with monstrous laugh.

"Now we need to kill Suggha and his brother Bhallad only to declare our rule in Kaalaghat." Mandha exclaimed.

"After the seventh day of the king's death, both brothers will go to graveyard to flower king's grave - this is wolves tradition. As soon as they will flower king's grave, we shower his grave with the blood of his sons."

Putani and Mandha, along with all other two-hundred hyenas, started dancing in frolic after listening to Lukata.

Hyenas were desperately waiting for the day, when Suggha and Bhallad would go to flower-the king's grave.

Eventually, one week had passed since the death of the Kaalaghat king; Kaalan and both of his sons were inching towards the graveyard. Lukata deployed ten hyenas in the graveyard, and they had camouflaged themselves and were eagerly waiting for Suggha and Bhallad. Lukata and her sisters were witnessing the scene from the horrible rocks at the border of Rock-field.

After flowering the king's grave, when Suggha and Bhallad turned to leave from there, they found themselves surrounded by ravenous hyenas. Wickedness and brutality were clearly visible in their eyes. Lukata and her sisters were about to come out, but around thirty wolves attacked on hyenas suddenly. Watching the situation in the favor of wolves, Lukata, Putani and Mandha left from there silently. Wolves killed all the ten hyenas in a sudden attack, as hyenas didn't get enough time to understand anything.

"How all this happened? Who transpired our plan to enemies?"

"Lukata, I think we cannot take Suggha and Bhallad for granted. Both of them are dangerous. We should have attacked on them with an impeccable strategy." Mandha exclaimed.

Lukata and Putani looked at Mandha with a look of approval. But Lukata was gasping in anger. After all, she had lost her ten hyenas in a well-planned clash.

Lukata would have declared hyenas rule in Kaalaghat, but Suggha came forward and managed wolves adeptly. Bhallad; was not much efficient in diplomacy, but he could do anything for his brother Suggha. Wolves did not want to decimate hyenas, but they wanted a peaceful ruling in Kaalaghat. Every animal in the jungle was very well aware of the wicked nature of the hyenas.

Hyenas issue forced all the animals of the jungle to gather outside Suggha's den to plan to keep hyenas away from the Kaalaghat throne. Wolves, jackals, deer, rabbits and many other animals were gathered. They all were discussing, but the solution of the hyena issue was not found.

Suddenly, the noise of the dry leaves arose out of the movements of some animals attracted attention of all the animals. They all stopped discussing and started staring towards the source of the sound. After some moments, Lukata with some other hyenas appeared there and came closer to all the gathered animals.

"Oh! I think, Kaalaghat throne discussion is going on." Lukata said sarcastically.

"Of course, if someone from outside will try to invade in our beautiful Kaalaghat, we do everything to keep them out." Bhallad said in anger.

"We are not trying to invade in Kaalghat, rather than we want to rule it- because we want Kaalghat throne to have the ruler with unlimited grit like king Kaalan." Lukata said in a serious tone.

"This is our problem. We don't want anyone from outside to interfere."

"No, Suggha this is not your problem only. We should keep humans in our brain always. One, who can keep humans at an arm's distance should rule a jungle - we are not saying that hyenas have more grit than you wolves, but selection of the ruler should be done fairly by giving a chance to the interested."

Listening to Lukata, wolves and all other animals were silent but looking thoughtful. Suddenly Bhaggu fox came up with a proposal for selection of the ruler.

"We should contest a dual fight between the leaders of both; hyenas and wolves." Bhaggu fox proposed.

All the animals were silent after listening to Bhaggu's proposal. Their silence turned into the agreement of Bhaggu fox proposal of a dual fight. They chose the day after the first rainfall for the selection of the Kaalaghat ruler. After that Lukata along with other hyenas, started moving towards her place in Rock-field.

"I am surprised that wolves did not oppose to dual fight." Putani said.

"They could not because of Lukata's strong points." Mandha said.

"Wolves are lucky that they did not object. If they had denied the proposal of a dual fight, then I would have killed all the wolves." Lukata said and grinned.

"But why you said that Kaalaghat needs a ruler with unlimited grit like Kaalan?" Mandha questioned.

"I said so to win the trust of other animals gathered there. Wolves must have understood my diplomacy, but others were swimming in the ocean of emotions."

The ring for dual fight was being prepared under the guidance of Bhaggu. The sky was clean but hyenas, wolves and all other animals were waiting for the first rain to fall desperately.

Fifteen days had passed without a single drop of rain, but on the sixteenth day, scorching sun was getting forbidden by the black clouds. The clouds were getting ready to drench the jungle, and sooner thunderstorms started giving warning to the jungle animals to remain indoors.

But Suggha, his brother Bhallad, and the other wolves were sitting silently near their den. All the wolves were looking stressful. The reason for their stress was Lukata; the villainous queen of hyenas.

"I only want peace between Kaalaghat and Rock-field. But, Lukata and her hyenas had started eyeing on Kaalaghat after the death of the king." Suggha broke the ice and said.

"We all know this very well, but this can only happen if hyenas maintain an arm's distance from the throne." an old wolf said.

"If the kingship of Kaalaghat goes in the hands of hyenas, everyone knows they will ruin the beauty of Kaalaghat. There will be no place for the law-abiding animals to hide their heads." other wolf said.

Bhallad and the other wolves agreed to the old wolf. The discussion amongst them was on when black clouds started drizzling.

"I am going to meet Lukata." said Suggha, after thinking about something.

"Why? I think there is no need to meet those ravenous hyenas." Bhallad cried in anger.

"I am going for some negotiation to avoid bloodshed."

The drizzle was getting furious and Suggha signaled to all the wolves to move inside their abodes. Then all the wolves started moving to their dens. But Suggha and Bhallad kept on sitting there. Both were looking deeply heedful. The furious rain was drenching both of them, but they had no care of themselves. Finally, Suggha got up and started inching towards Rock-field, but he asked Bhallad to go inside the den. Bhallad tried to stop Suggha, but he turned a deaf ear to him and moved to meet Lukata.

After some moments, when Suggha reached Lukata's place, he saw Lukata eating the flesh of a baby deer. Other hyenas were looking at Suggha in wrath. Lukata stared at Suggha, but said nothing and kept on eating. After finishing the flesh of a baby deer, Lukata got up and licked her mouth with her tongue. But the blood of the baby deer was still there on her face.

"What brought you inside the Rock-field?" Lukata asked in anger.

"Lukata, you are happy in your Rock-field and we are happy in our Kaalaghat. We never look at your Rock-field, then why are you eyeing Kaalaghat?"

"You cannot even dream of eyeing Rock-field. Because wolves don't have grit. But we will rule in Kaalaghat."

"Lukata! you are wrong. I wanted a peaceful life for you, but you are choosing the wrong path."

"Suggha, do not think too much about hyenas peace, it is my task. Go from here, and rather than wasting your time in search of hyenas peace, prepare for fight."

"Okay! be prepared Lukata - now we will meet tomorrow in the ring, in front of everyone."

Then, Suggha left from there. All the hyenas along with Lukata kept on watching Suggha until he was disappeared.

Suggha reached at his place, water from his body was dribbling, as rain drenched him completely, and he was looking lethargic.

"So, how was the meeting with your dear Lukata?" Bhallad asked in anger.

"Leave it. Now, I will have to win the fight, anyhow. They cannot understand the language of serenity. Only kingship can forbid them from spreading terror and bloodshed in Kaalaghat." Suggha said and jerked his body to get rid of the rainwater.

"I already told you, but you wanted to teach them the lesson of peace, who cannot understand the language of serenity - we have to teach them in the language, they understand, and this can be done only after becoming the ruler."

Suggha nodded and laid down inside the den. Rain was still on, and raining water was playing the role of love threads between the jungle and the black clouds.

Bhallad also laid down, thinking about the next morning. Several thoughts were circulating in Bhallad's brain; about the throne; about the animals of Kaalaghat jungle; the ring for a dual fight; and many more. Lost in those thoughts, Bhallad got slept.

In the later part of night, Bhallad woke up suddenly with the sound of a thunderstorm, and he called Suggha, but there was no response. Then he got up and looked for Suggha, but he was not there inside the den. Then Bhallad came outside the den, but Suggha was also not there. He called all the other wolves in his typical voice. All the wolves gathered in a jiffy, but Suggha was missing. The signs of worries and tension were clearly visible on the faces of the wolves. After-all, their leader was missing just before a dual fight.

Fortunately, the rain stopped in some time and all the wolves started looking for Suggha. They kept on looking for Suggha till morning, but neither they could find him nor any clue. Finally, a short meeting amongst wolves was convened, and all the wolves decided Bhallad to fight with Lukata in the ring.

In the morning, again black clouds started making love with jungle. There was a complete darkness in the jungle. All the wolves, all the hyenas, jackals, deer and many other animals and birds were gathered near the ring to witness the fight. All were looking enthusiastic.

As Bhallad reached inside the ring, wolves started chanting his name to boost his morale, but moxie was missing somewhere within them. After a bit, Lukata also pounced into the ring, and a wave of moxie propagated through the hyenas after watching Lukata in the ring, and they were being rambunctious and started making hubbub. Hyenas were looking more confidant for Lukata's win, as Suggha was not there in the ring opposite to Lukata. Rain was on wild mode and it was drenching every corner of the jungle. The icy wind was blowing through the Kaalaghat to witness the fight for the throne. Finally, Lukata and Bhallad were standing in the ring, facing each other.

"Where is the absconder Suggha?….. Ohhh, he has no grit to face Lukata, so he must have made you a scapegoat- he has not sent you to face me rather than to meet your death." Lukata laughed like a monster, and bombarded sarcastic comments on Bhallad. But Bhallad did not reply, and he was looking melancholic.

The chances of wolves to win the kingship were dwindling in the absence of Suggha, and the time was getting idyllic for the hyenas.

Finally, all the animals cried altogether for three times, and the fight between Lukata and Bhallad started. Lukata was in attacking mode and Bhallad was trying to thwart the attacks of Lukata. Bhallad's body was present in the ring, but he was looking lost somewhere else. Noticing Bhallad fighting with no enthusiasm, wolves and some other animals started chanting his name to boost his morale. After that, Bhallad started fighting aggressively. Both were fighting bravely, and Bhallad was having the upper hand in the fight and wounded Lukata. He tried to grab the Lukata's neck several times, but every time she got a narrow-escape. A goose-bumping fight was going on, when misfortune for wolves happened. Bhallad got slipped because of the slippery land, and his neck was just before Lukata's jaws. She did not waste her time in thinking, and grabbed his neck in her jaws. Blood started dribbling profusely from Bhallad's neck, and he was trying to get rid of. Lukata did not weaken her grab, and Bhallad started crying because of exquisite pain. Lukata kept on biting his neck, and finally she left Bhallad, only when wolves accepted their defeat.

Shoulders of wolves were down, and they left from there with woebegone expressions on their faces, but Lukata received the plaudits of hyenas for winning the throne of Kaalaghat. Bhallad was leaving with the pack of wolves, but his moves were looking languished. All were heading towards their places in the Kaalaghat jungle.

One week passed under appalling conditions in the Kaalaghat jungle. Wolves under the leadership of Bhallad left no stone un-turned to find Suggha, but they could not get any fruitful result.

"Congratulations to all the hyenas for being the ruler of Kaalaghat." Lukata cried loudly. Listening to that, all the hyenas started crying in joy.

"Bhallad and his wolves army may create obstruction in our ruling." Mandha said.

"Wolves always abide by the jungle rules. So, they will not create any obstruction. One week has passed since we became the ruler, but the feeling of winning the Kaalaghat throne is missing. Just do one thing- enjoy hunting and spread hyenas's terror in every corner of Kaalaghat Jungle." Lukata ordered.

Suddenly, almost fifty hyenas moved from Rock-field and attacked on rabbits in Kaalaghat. Until rabbits got into a safer zone, hyenas hunted and decimated their population in Kaalaghat. After playing bloodshed, hyenas ate them up to their throats and returned to Rock-field with killed rabbits in their mouths. All the survival rabbits were quivering after witnessing hyenas brutality. But, to hide themselves was not the ultimate solution, so they transpired the heinous act of hyenas to Bhallad.

A group of rabbits in stress reached to meet Bhallad, and explained him everything. Bhallad was extremely livid with the brutal act of the hyenas. Suddenly, Bhallad with his some other wolves got up and moved towards Rock-field to meet Lukata for their heinous act against rabbits.

Lukata and other hyenas were relishing the flesh of freshly killed rabbits when Bhallad and other wolves reached. "How dared you to play bloodshed in Kaalaghat and kill rabbits?" blood over there rankled Bhallad, and he screamed in ire.

"Bhallad, I am surprised that how you dared to ask me this question! Even you know hyenas are nonpareil in playing bloodshed. We can dare to do anything in Kaalaghat, whatever we want. We will rule the Kaalaghat in our typical style- do not forget that wolves are no more the ruler of the Kaalaghat."

The venomous remarks of Lukata had tectonic effects on the wolves and made Bhallad discombobulated. He could not respond to Lukata's venomous remarks. Despite feeling ashamed, Bhallad warned hyenas about adverse consequences if they play bloodshed in Kaalaghat again. After that, Bhallad turned to leave from there and all the other wolves were following Bhallad. Hyenas were chuckling behind the wolves.

Bhallad asked the rabbits to return to their place and assured them that hyenas would not play bloodshed in Kaalaghat again. He further warned the rabbits to be more cautious, as hyenas were not trustworthy. Rabbits left from there with lugubrious faces and moved towards their place.

In the night, Bhallad was sitting alone inside the den, and he was praying to God for Suggha with teary eyes.

"God!, where is Suggha? .... Without him, I am alone and cannot control these nefarious hyenas. When he was with us, it was looking too easy to maintain the camaraderie and tranquility in Kaalaghat. But without him, everything is looking impossible. Nothing is going good.

Kaalaghat is calling him. Kaalaghat needs Suggha. Please God! send Suggha back to save these helpless animals from these unruly hyenas. God! I do not know even why Suggha left us? What mistake I made, Suggha left us saying nothing.... Please God, do something. If not for me, then please do it, at least for Kaalaghat."

After offering prayer to God, Bhallad closed his eyes and tried to sleep, but he could not sleep for hours. A lot of notions regarding Suggha and Kaalaghat were circulating in his brain. Finally, he came out of the den and sat down under the giant Banyan tree. Tears were coming out of his eyes. Bhaggu was passing by, and he noticed Bhallad weeping. He stopped and came to him.

"Come Bhaggu, why are you roaming so late?"

"Today, I could not sleep after getting the news of the massacre of the rabbits. So, I thought to take a round to feel better."

"Do not roam alone for some days until we get legit control over hyenas. So, be careful." Both kept on talking for long.

"In the late evening, I have seen two hyenas going towards the western side. Both were following Lukata, and one of them was carrying a loaf of flesh in his jaws." Bhaggu said with a gloomy look.

"Lukata's ultimate target is to spread terror amongst the Kaalaghat animals. We will have to dethrone hyenas from Kaalaghat throne soon."

Bhaggu nodded, and after some moments he got up, yawned and moved from there. Bhallad kept on watching him from behind. Then, Bhallad also got up and entered inside the den and laid down to sleep.

Next day, Bhallad woke up in the morning. He came out of the den and he was looking very heedful. Suddenly, he called all the wolves with his typical sound. Other wolves gathered under the dense Banyan tree in a jiffy.

"In the night, Bhaggu fox was passing by, and I was sitting here. He approached me and we had a conversation for a long duration."

"Is this the reason for calling us urgently?" Chhedi wolf asked in wonder.

"No! but, during the conversation, Bhaggu told a very important thing. He told that he had seen Lukata with two hyenas with a loaf of flesh in one's mouth, in the late evening moving towards the west side of the jungle. For whom they carried that loaf of flesh?"

"We will have to spy the hyenas." Chhedi said in wonder.

"Yes, from today evening, deploy at least a team of 10 wolves to spy hyenas." Bhallad ordered Chhedi.

In the evening, chilly breeze was passing through the Kaalaghat, from one end to another. Black clouds were trying to bar the moon, but it was peeping intermittently. Ten wolves camouflaged themselves near the way, to the western part of the Kaalaghat, for spying the hyenas. They kept on waiting for three-four hours, but their wait was not getting over. Finally, they were about to leave when they heard the hyenas suddenly. They saw Lukata followed by two hyenas, moving towards the west. One hyena was moving with a loaf of flesh in her mouth, as Bhaggu explained to Bhallad earlier in the night. Hyenas passed wolves without noticing them, as they had camouflaged themselves in toto. The team of ten wolves started following hyenas clandestinely and silently. Wolves kept on following hyenas, and after some time Lukata and her hyenas stopped near a temporary structure made of bamboos.

There were a lot of horned owls sitting on a giant mango tree outside that structure. Wolves were noticing everything. Lukata was talking to the main horned owl; Lalla, but wolves could not listen to their conversation because of being at some distance and the noise of the tree leaves causing by the icy breeze. So, wolves moved closer to hyenas to listen to them properly. They were getting closer silently, but suddenly Lalla noticed them, and cried in his typical sound. Listening to Lalla, all the horned owls attacked on wolves. The team of ten wolves was getting it difficult to cope with owls, as they were air striking on wolves. The wolves-owls battle was a great show for Lukata and other hyenas. But hyenas completely dumbfounded wolves, as around fifty hyenas were around them. They all were licking their mouths with their tongues. They all were waiting for Lukata's signal for the deadly attack.

"Fools! you must be thinking that wolves were following hyenas; but the reality is just contrary. You wolves were being followed by your death; hyenas." Lukata came closer to wolves and said with monstrous laugh.

Wolves understood only God could save them, so they looked at each other and decided to flee from there, as they could not face the army of fifty hyenas. Suddenly, they started fleeing from there in all directions, but hyenas were already alert. Not even a single wolf could escape, but they killed two hyenas. But the hyenas have slaughtered all the ten wolves. Hyenas collected the dead bodies of wolves in one place.

"We will keep on decimating the wolves like this, and a day will follow when Kaalaghat will be wolf-free." Lukata's tone was serious. Other hyenas started eating bodies of wolves in such an obnoxious way, as they were facing hunger for decades. After finishing all the work, the remaining hyenas also left for Rock-field. Lalla with other horned-owls was again sitting on the mango tree to guard the bamboo structure.

Later at night, Bhallad and the other wolves were sitting outside the den. All were looking stressful, as their brother wolves did not return. Bhaggu was also sitting mournfully. Bhallad and the other wolves were getting restless.

"We should go towards the western side of the Kaalaghat, in maximum number, to look for our brothers. I feel that they all are in deep trouble."

"Bhallad, I think we should wait for them till morning. This might be a trap for us, and if unfortunately I am right, brutal hyenas will not miss the boat to decimate us." Bhaggu said worriedly.

All other wolves agreed with Bhaggu, so Bhallad had to postpone the search until morning.

Lukata and other hyenas were enjoying in Rock-field. They all were dancing like mads. Sufficient flesh of rabbits was available there on the platter.

"Wolves were out at night to solve the bamboo - structure mystery, but look at their destiny - they got another mystery of lost wolves to solve. This shows that wolves are not worthy of becoming the ruler of Kaalaghat."

All the hyenas started laughing after listening to Lukata.

Next morning, when Bhallad and Bhaggu with other wolves visited the west side of the Kaalaghat, they did not get even a single trace of lost wolves.

All were scratching their heads after a futile chase to search the lost wolves. Hyenas had enough time in the night to clear the remnant of the dead bodies of wolves.

A multicolored peacock; Bakota was noticing everything from behind the bushes. The melancholic faces of Bhallad and other wolves forced him to talk to them. Bakota came out from behind the bushes and stopped near Bhallad.

"What happened? Why are you all roaming with gloomy faces?" Bakota asked.

Then Bhallad explained him everything about the lost wolves, and tears started dribbling from his eyes. "Bhallad, it is really a sad and goose-bumping incident. But, do not worry, things will change and good time reaches soon."

Then Bakota squawked and flew towards the southern part of the Kaalaghat.

"Bakota is not trustworthy. He is villainous. He lives in Kaalaghat with only his family of three members, but he decimated all the members of the family of Dhameena snake in the jungle." Bhaggu said in a complaining tone. "We should move now. I think, We have lost our wolf brothers like Suggha. Nothing is going well for us." Bhallad said and started moving back. All the other wolves were following him. All faces were looking dejected and hopeless.

In the night, Bhallad was sitting alone with a gloomy face inside the den. Suddenly, he listened to someone calling his name very softly from outside the den. Bhallad got up and came out of the den. He saw the Bakota peacock out of the den..

"Bakota! this time you are here! What happened?"

"First, let me allow to come inside your den, then I will explain everything. Had someone seen me with you, then there would be a troublesome situation for me and my family."

"Yes Bakota, come inside."

Bakota rushed inside the den, and Bhallad looked around, then he also entered inside the den. Bhallad looking at Bakota.

"I do not know if you are going to believe me because of my tarnished reputation in Kaalaghat."

Bhallad said nothing, but kept on staring at him. Bakota looked around and came closer to Bhallad.

"What I am going to say, please do not share it with Bhaggu."

"The lost wolves, whom you all were looking for today, are not alive anymore. Lukata and her hyenas slaughtered them all."

Listening to that, Bhallad pounced upon Bakota in anger. Bakota fell supine on the ground, and his neck was under Bhallad's grab.

"What nonsense you are talking!"

"Because I have witnessed their massacre. I was passing by when hyenas were killing wolves."

"Why should I believe you?"

"I don't know, but I do not have any reason to lie. You should believe me."

After thinking for a while, Bhallad loosen his grab and Bakota got up, but he was looking terrified. His beak and eyes were wide opened, and he was gasping in fear. "I'm sorry Bakota. My mind is not working. I do not understand diplomacy enough. I really do not know how to wriggle out of all this."

"I can understand your mental status. But I am with you. I will not only tell you everything what I know, but also help you."

"Where I met you today in the western side of the jungle, I always see some hyenas coming and going. There must be something important you should know; especially that small bamboo structure." Bakota informed.

"But there was no such structure we noticed when visited today."

"Because hyenas always hide that behind a plethora amount of wood and leaves. Hyenas deployed an army of horned owls for guarding that area in the night."

"What about the security in the day, as we had seen no horned owls?"

"In the day, horned owls handover the security to vultures."

Bhallad was thinking about making a plan to enter inside the bamboo prison.

"I will help you out. Only I need six to seven wolves to flummox horned owls. But their lives may be in danger."

"How you will do this, and why you are helping us to this extent?"

"Don't worry, Bhallad, I will do this, whether I have to sacrifice my life. Once, king Kaalan had saved my family from Dhameena snake, so it is my duty not only to inform you but also to help you."

Then, after both had fixed the coming evening for their operation, when there will be no hyena near the bamboo prison.

"Only those two hours will be convenient for deviating horned owls and to know the secrets of the bamboo structure" Bakota said.

Bhallad nodded. Then, Bakota came out of the den silently and flew from there towards his family in the western part of the Kaalaghat.

Next evening, Eight wolves gathered under the Banyan tree, and Bhallad explained them everything. When night was falling, they all left from there towards the bamboo structure. They were moving silently and clandestinely to avoid themselves to be noticed. Finally, they almost reached near the place where bamboo structure was situated. Bakota was already there, waiting for the wolves. He stopped them and explained to them the plan of action. Then Bakota moved from there, and wolves started running towards the bamboo structure suddenly. Watching wolves running towards the bamboo structure, the horned owls got bemused, and they all attacked on wolves to scatter them. Watching all the horned owls busy with wolves, Bakota rushed, opened the gate and entered inside the bamboo structure. He locked the gate of the structure from inside.

A battle between wolves and horned owls was going on, and after sometime Bakota flew from there squawking. Bakota's squawk was the signal for the wolves to leave from there. Listening to Bakota's squawk, all the wolves started fleeing towards their place, and owls thought they were fleeing because of the fear of defeat. All wolves returned safely, but the horned owl's attack wounded two wolves.

As wolves reached, Bhallad asked them to go to relax. The wolves moved their dens to relax, and Bhallad also went inside his den. He was waiting for Bakota and time was getting heavier in wait for Bakota.

When Lukata, along with Putani and Mandha, reached
the bamboo prison, Lalla; leader of the horned owls,
informed her about the sudden attack of wolves.

"That must be a planned attack. You should have sent
any of you to inform us. But….. Because of you fools, we
missed an opportunity to kill some more wolves. We would
have made this ground a graveyard for them." Lukata
thought for a while and cried. All the horned owls were
kept on listening to Lukata silently and submissively.

"Next time don't make any mistake. If they come, just
send anyone to inform us." Lukata said and threw the rabbit
flesh towards owls in wrath and left from there.

Bakota was noticing everything from hiding himself in
the bushes. As hyenas left, Bakota also took the aerial route
towards Bhallad's place. When Bakota reached, Bhallad
was waiting desperately for him outside the den. Both
entered inside the den after looking around.

"Bakota, please tell me about the secrets of bamboo
structure."

"When I entered inside the bamboo structure, I could
not believe whatever my eyes had seen. I had seen Suggha.
His hands and legs were bound tightly. He was looking
frail. Wounds on his body have become festered."

After listening to Bakota, tears started dribbling from
the eyes of Bhallad.

"Why did you not inform us that time? We would get
our Suggha free from their control that time."

"It was not possible. Trying to free Suggha was like
putting his life at stake."

"Did Suggha inform you that how he reached in hyenas
grab?"

"Yes, he explained me the story of his abduction."

"Bhallad, remember that scary night just before the day of a dual fight for Kaalaghat throne."

That night, rain was on wild mode and you were sleeping inside the den, but Suggha was asleep. He had to face head-to-head fight with Lukata for the Kaalaghat throne. Suggha wanted to take blessings of the martyred king of Kaalaghat; Kaalan, so he got up and left towards Kaalan's grave silently in the rain. He looked around and started moving towards the king Kaalan's grave. He was moving and wild rain was drenching him.

Finally, he reached and sat near the grave. He was looking melancholic and tears were dribbling from his eyes. The raining threads of water were wiping his tears. After praying and taking blessings, Suggha got up and turned to move towards the den. But, he got himself surrounded by wicked Lukata and other hyenas. They all were staring at Suggha, and their motive was quite clear in their reddish eyes. Then Lukata came closer to Suggha and stood face to face, chuckling.

"So, have you taken the blessings of dead Kaalan?" Lukata commented sarcastically.

"Don't take the name of martyred king with your dirty tongue." Suggha screamed in anger.

"Oh! this much anger does not suit on you, Suggha. Anger and game of blood suit only on hyenas."

"Why you are here? What do you want?"

"Until you are there with wolves, the chances of hyenas to rule the Kaalaghat are dwindling. So, we are here to avert your presence in the ring tomorrow."

"Lukata, at least show some loyalty and honesty despite having ill-will for Kaalaghat."

"We hyenas do not believe in loyalty and honesty, rather than we believe in supreme power." Lukata said and signaled other hyenas to capture Suggha.

Suddenly, hyenas pounced on Suggha and captured him.

"Suggha, don't worry, we would not kill you, rather than we will keep you alive in our prison. We would give you a chance to witness the decimation of Bhallad and all the other wolves. I will make you to feel the real revenge of our dead hyenas; you wolves had killed on the king's grave flowering day".

Suggha was crying in anger, but hyenas took him with them inside the Rock-field.

Bhallad and Bakota, both were weeping.

"But they imprisoned Suggha in Kaalaghat, not in Rock-field!" Bhallad asked in surprise.

"After winning the Kaalaghat throne, Lukata shifted Suggha to Kaalaghat from Rock-field" Bakota replied.

"We would attack on hyenas, and get Suggha free from their imprisonment right now." Bhallad screamed furiously.

"No, Bhallad, we have to make an impeccable plan to take on hyenas. We cannot take chances, after-all Suggha is in hyenas prison."

Listening to Bakota, Bhallad became thoughtful. Watching Bhallad lost in thoughts, Bakota looked outside the den.

"I think, It's too late now, and I should leave now. We will ponder over it tomorrow." Bakota said.

"Ok Bakota, be careful. We will meet tomorrow."

Then, after looking around cautiously, Bakota flew towards his family in the west.

When Bakota reached at his place, nobody was at his home. He started quacking and looking around in a haste. Suddenly, he noticed Bhaggu staring and chuckling at him. He tended towards Bhaggu with cautious moves.

"What do you think? You can convene meetings with wolves unnoticed! Bakota, your every move was being monitored." Bhaggu said with a mischievous smile.

"Bhaggu! Where is my family?"

"When hyenas don't harm your family and there is no enmity between you and hyenas, then what forced you to play the political game against hyenas?"

"I am not playing any political game. It is your business. You are backstabbing Bhallad and wolves. You were always doubtful. But I am just supporting the truth."

"Ok, then go to Lukata and crawl for the life of your family, which is performing a very attractive dance at Lukata's place." Bhaggu said and laughed brazenly.

Listening to that, Bakota suddenly flew towards Lukata's place and Bhaggu followed him.

Bakota saw his family dancing before the nefarious hyenas. His wife was crawling before Lukata for freedom. But Lukata and other hyenas were busy in watching the dance of the Bakota's family. Bakota could not rely on his eyes.

"Lukata! leave my family. They are innocent. If I did anything wrong, kill me." Bakota screamed in ire.

"Please tell him, who does the right things, is the biggest enemy of hyenas." Lukata looked at Mandha and said.

"We forgive no one who tries to stand against the hyenas. But, I give you an opportunity to rectify your mistake." Lukata said.

"What opportunity?" asked Bakota.

"If you agree to support us in all aspects, I will let your family go free." Lukata offered.

"Do not think that I am Bhaggu. He may accept your slavery, but I……"

Lukata attacked on Bakota suddenly and killed him, before he could answer. Other hyenas also attacked on Bakota's family, and all the members of his family were lying dead in a jiffy.

"This was inevitable, especially when someone is trying to dance against hyenas." Bhaggu looked at Bakota's dead body and murmured.

"When Bakota supported Bhallad and wolves, the death of his entire family was scripted. I wanted him to cash the opportunity to save his family by supporting hyenas, but…. the stupid jungle dancer was trying to play a leader. He was trying to play the political game against hyenas." cleaning the Bakota's blood on her mouth, cried Lukata.

Next evening, Bhallad and other wolves were desperately waiting for Bakota. Time was passing, and Bakota's non-arrival was making wolves restless. Bhaggu was also pretending to be restless.

"I think there is something wrong with Bakota. He must be in some adverse situation. I am going to look for him." Bhaggu said worriedly.

Bhallad asked some wolves to accompany Bhaggu for his safety, but Bhaggu persuaded Bhallad and moved alone.

Bhallad pretended to be persuaded, but a lot of thoughts about Bhaggu were circulating in his brain. The countless positive and negative thoughts made a cobweb in Bhallad's brain. But Bhallad kept those thoughts secretive in his mind, and did not share with anyone; even with his minion wolves. After sometime, Bhallad asked the Bhaggu's family and all other wolves to leave him alone. Then Bhaggu's family and all the other wolves stood up and left from there. Bhallad was sitting alone outside the den. He was waiting for Bhaggu and for Bakota, but Bhaggu was busy with hyenas.

"….. and stupid Bhallad and wolves are waiting for Bakota." laughingly said Bhaggu.

"Just inform Bhallad about the brutal killing of Bakota and his family, and also ask him to arrange a condolence meet for Bakota." Lukata laughed monstrously and said.

Bhaggu got up to leave, but Lukata stopped him and asked to take his reward. Then Putani threw a loaf of fish towards Bhaggu, and he grabbed the loaf and left from there enthusiastically. Bhaggu's mouth was watering, so he swallowed the whole loaf.

"For such free loafs without working, I am doing all this." Bhaggu said to himself and kept on moving. As Bhaggu was about to reach to Bhallad, he started running to show his pseudo loyalty to Bhallad. In some time Bhaggu reached to Bhallad. He was gasping badly.

"What happened? Why are you gasping badly?" questioned Bhallad.

"Hyenas have killed the whole family of Bakota." with teary eyes said Bhaggu.

"Now, hyenas have crossed all the limits. They have to face the consequences."

The anger was quite visible in Bhallad's reddish eyes. Other wolves gathered at once with the piercing sound of Bhallad.

"Today, in the night, we will attack on hyenas, and teach them the lesson of revenge."

After some moments, Bhallad went inside the den, and all the other wolves also left from there. Bhaggu also left from there with a pretentious gloomy face.

After an hour, Bhaggu came and looked around and moved towards Rock-field silently to meet Lukata again. He informed hyenas that wolves would attack on hyenas in the night.

"We will wait for wolves attack. Today will be the last day of wolves existence in Kaalaghat." cried Lukata.

After transpiring the information, Bhaggu left from there, and he did not realize that he was being followed by four wolves. On the way, the wolves came closer to Bhaggu.

"From where you are returning Bhaggu?" one wolf asked.

"From nowhere. I just went in search of some food for my kids."

"Ok! let us move faster. Bhallad was looking for you to make some strategy for night attack." other wolf said.

Then Bhaggu and all the four wolves started moving faster. Bhallad and all the wolves were waiting for them outside the den. After some time, Bhaggu accompanied by four hyenas reached near the den.

"Bhallad, your doubt as right. Bhaggu is living in Kaalghat, but he is working for hyenas. He has informed Lukata about our night attack on hyenas." wolves informed Bhallad. Listening to that, Bhaggu tried to flee, but the wolves grabbed him.

"We will not attack on hyenas. I gave the wrong information for checking your loyalty. Bhaggu, your loyalty is pure, but unfortunately, it is on the wrong side. Because of you, we lost Bakota and his family. Because of you, Suggha is not with us. We took thee at the world, and you have broken our reliance." Bhallad said with a gloomy face.

"You will have to pay for all the losses. Wolves have suffered a lot because of you." further added Bhallad. Then he ordered to capture Bhaggu. He started crawling for his freedom, but wolves turned their deaf ear to Bhaggu, and imprisoned him.

"We will leave you alive, if you agree to do one task for us." Bhallad asked after thinking something. "I will do anything, whatever you ask." replied Bhaggu.

"Wait for the right time, and remember not to befool us again, otherwise your family will face the consequences."

"No, I will do everything. But do not harm my family."

Bhaggu was weeping, but wolves turned their deaf ears towards him. All the wolves were sitting together.

"Now we cannot wait anymore. We have to get Suggha free from hyenas prison." said Bhallad.

"We have to attack on hyenas in full strength." one old wolf said.

"Let us make an impeccable plan before attacking on hyenas. In the night, we will decide about our attack." thought something for a while and said Bhallad.

In the mid-night, Bhallad came out of his den, and went to king Kaalan's grave in the graveyard. Almost fifty wolves were covering him. Bhallad went near the grave alone, and the rest of the wolves were standing at an arm's distance.

"Lord! Please show me the right path, so I can save Kaalaghat and Suggha from these villainous hyenas without their massacre." Bhallad prayed and closed his eyes.

Then king Kaalan appeared in his awakening dream.

"I know, you are kind-hearted. You do not want to kill the whole species of hyenas. But, they will kill all the animals, and destroy the beauty of Kaalaghat. It is your duty to kill all the hyenas to save all the other animals. It is your duty to save the beauty of Kaalaghat. So, do not ponder too much, and take on hyenas to save Kaalaghat. It is your responsibility to free Kaalaghat with the terror of the hyenas."

Suddenly, Bhallad woke up and opened his eyes, but king Kaalan was not there. Bhallad looked around and cried 'king- king' many times, but there was complete silence. Other wolves got bemused after listening Bhallad. They informed Bhallad that there was nobody in the graveyard. After listening to wolves, Bhallad smiled and kissed the Kaalan's grave and left from there.

Bhaggu was sitting in the prison with a gloomy face, and Bhallad was sitting with all the wolves. Bhallad allowed Bhaggu to listen to the wolves during the conversation. Bhallad decided to attack on hyenas in the next night.

"Have you thought about the strategy?" one wolf asked. Bhallad looked at him in surprise, but said nothing.

"Our one hundred wolves will attack on Rock-field, and the remaining wolves would go to the west to get Suggha free." Bhallad said.

"What is the need of sending so many wolves to get Suggha free? This strategy will weaken our major force in front of the hyenas" another wolf said.

"I have already thought about this. Lukata always tried to play the 'divide-strategy' with wolves, but this time her own strategy will vanish hyenas not only from Kaalaghat but also from Rock-field."

Listening to Bhallad, all the wolves became enthusiastic. Then, Bhallad asked all the wolves to leave for the night to get prepared for the next night. All the wolves left from there with pleasant faces. Bhallad also entered inside his den, and he was thinking about the time he had spent with Suggha.

He was smiling, but tears were there in his eyes. Lost in those thoughts, Bhallad got slept.

Next morning, Bhallad and his wolves army were gathered, and waiting for the night to attack on hyenas.

"First, we all will attack on hyenas, and except Lukata, we should leave no hyena alive, no matter how many wolves have to sacrifice their lives for this." said Bhallad.

"Why should we leave Lukata alive?" one wolf asked.

"I have thought something about that wicked Lukata, so her life is very important to me."

Then, Bhallad asked wolves to free Bhaggu. One wolf moved ahead and freed him. Bhaggu came to Bhallad and started crawling for the life of his and his family.

"We will decide the future of your family after today's ultimate battle with hyenas. So, go to hyenas and reveal our plan to them."

Listening to that, Bhaggu was dumbfounded. "But…. if I reveal the strategy to hyenas, then how wolves will become victorious?"

"Just inform, this is also a part of our strategy…., and do not forget that life of your family is in our hands." Bhallad reminded Bhaggu.

"I will do whatever you said." Bhaggu said and moved towards Rock-field. Bhaggu informed Lukata about the wolves attack, and he also informed Lukata about the complete strategy.

"If this is true, we will have to divide our army, and we will become weaker." Putani said worriedly.

"Do not worry, if we split, then definitely, we are going to vanish. But, we will not split." Lukata said.

"But how? We are only Two hundred hyenas, and we will have to deploy one hundred hyenas in the west in Kaalaghat, where we imprisoned Suggha." said Mandha.

"You will always remain a fool like wolves. We will shift Suggha here in Rock-field from Kaalaghat right now. Then there would be no need to split our army." Lukata said.

Bhallad, with his all wolves army, was approaching towards the bamboo prison, and they had surrounded all that area clandestinely.

"Are you sure that Lukata would shift Suggha from here?" one wolf asked.

"If the fate is with us, then Lukata will definitely shift Suggha from here to avoid her army's division……, and this time fate is with Kaalaghat, and Kaalaghat is with us." said Bhallad.

Out of two hundred hyenas, Lukata sent around one hundred hyenas to the west to bring Suggha. They stood up and started approaching towards Kaalaghat. Bhaggu was also with them. Hyenas were moving in full enthusiasm, but Bhaggu; with a woebegone face. After sometime, hyenas started running, and dust on the way started flying. Flying dust was showing towards some inevitable and horrifying incident in the offing in Kaalaghat.

After some moments, wolves noticed the flying dust, which was showing the heroic arrival of the rivals. Bhallad was getting excited to see Suggha.

"No one will attack on hyenas, until they bring Suggha outside of the prison" instructed Bhallad.

"We will allow hyenas to bring Suggha outside, and as soon as they will about to leave from here, we will attack on them from every direction" further added Bhallad.

Suddenly, the wolves scattered and deployed themselves all around. In a while, an army of hyenas reached at the spot. Mannu, the leader of vultures, came down from the tree to greet the hyenas.

"We are taking Suggha to our place, so your security services are no more required for us. Mannu, you can leave now with all your vultures." Putani said.

"Ok! ask Lukata to meet me, whenever you require security services." Mannu said and asked the other vultures to vacate the tree. They all flew from there, creating hubbub.

Hyenas were totally unaware of the wolves presence around them behind the dense bushes. Then six hyenas entered inside the prison, and rest were waiting outside. Bhallad's heart-beats were increasing uncontrollably. He was trying to be calm, but every single second, he was getting impossible to pass. Finally, six hyenas; who entered inside the prison, came out, and Suggha was with them. They tied him with many ropes. He became too frail, that he was finding almost impossible to move on his own. His bones were quite visible, and he was seeming almost like a skeleton. Bhallad's eyes were filled with tears, and he was quivering in anger. Hyenas started moving, and they were dragging Suggha with the help of the ropes.

Suddenly, wolves attacked on hyenas from all directions. Before hyenas could understand anything, wolves killed many hyenas and freed Suggha from hyenas. Bhallad deployed around fifty wolves for Suggha's security. They were not participating in the battle, but were safeguarding Suggha. Rest of the wolves were killing hyenas. The battle was going on, and hyenas were also attacking on wolves, but they were fewer in numbers than of wolves. Bhallad and wolves were killing them mercilessly. The ground became red because of the blood. Wolves killed every single hyena, as they did not leave any space uncovered for hyenas to flee. However, almost Fifteen wolves had to succumb to death in the battle. The faces of the wolves became red with the blood of hyenas. After that, Bhallad and all the other wolves brought Suggha with them to their den. Bhaggu was also with them, as he did not go to Lukata.

Lukata was waiting for hyenas and Suggha desperately. She was moving in to-fro motion. Time was passing, as it had wings, but there was no trace of hyenas return.

Bhallad called Dr. Furti to check the health of Suggha. He was checking Suggha meticulously, and Suggha was trying to speak something, but he was finding it difficult to speak up anything. The condition of Suggha was seemingly worrisome. Watching the condition of Suggha, Bhallad and the other wolves started weeping. "Do not worry, he will be fine in some days, but hyenas tortured Suggha up-to the maximum level." said doctor Furti.

Mannu was flying over west, and suddenly he looked at a lot of dead bodies lying on the ground. He landed at once cautiously; noticed the dead bodies of hyenas, and got bemused. So, he flew towards Lukata in Rock-field, and informed her about the scene in Kaalaghat.

Lukata was crying like a mad in anger.

"I will not leave any wolf alive in Kaalaghat. Before they could attack on us, we would attack on wolves." cried Lukata.

"But now we are very fewer compared to wolves. They have succeeded in their agenda." one hyena said.

But Lukata was getting mad after listening to Mannu.

"We will attack on wolves right now, and remember one thing, if we are going to lose this battle, we will kill Suggha and Bhallad anyhow." cried Lukata.

All the hyenas started running towards Kaalaghat for the last clash.

"The work is half done, still Lukata and almost one hundred hyenas are alive in Rock-field. We will have to sabotage the whole species of hyenas for the welfare of all the animals in Kaalaghat" Bhallad said.

They were about to move towards hyenas place, but hyenas attacked on wolves suddenly. About twenty wolves took their position at the entrance of the den to cover Suggha, as he was inside the den. Rest of the wolves were fighting with hyenas. In a sudden attack, hyenas killed about thirty wolves in a jiffy.

"After massacring you wolves, I will kill Bhaggu with his family. After all, because of him you could kill our hyenas." cried Lukata after watching Bhaggu with wolves. "Lukata! don't dream of killing all the wolves. We wanted peace in Kaalaghat, so we were crawling in front of you. But, you took us for granted and started killing helpless animals, and disturbed the peace in Kaalaghat. But, you never realized that we can also play bloodshed for the establishment of the peace." Bhallad cried.

The battle full of blood was going on, and wolves were killing hyenas. Only some hyenas remained alive, and they were fighting with wolves. Hyenas also killed about fifty wolves and wounded around thirty.

Suddenly, Bhallad attacked on Lukata, and grabbed her neck. She fell down screaming, and Bhallad's deadly attack stopped her movements. The wolves had sabotaged the whole species of hyenas for the establishment of peace. All the wolves gathered and started segregating dead bodies of wolves from the heap of the dead bodies of both; hyenas and wolves.

Lukata looked towards the entrance of the den with her half squinted eyes. Noticing the entrance with no guarding, she got up and pounced inside the den suddenly. She did not waste any time and attacked on Suggha. Before Bhallad could reach inside the den, Lukata killed frail Suggha in a jiffy.

Bhallad was crying after watching the dead body of Suggha, but Lukata was laughing like a monster. Next moment, Bhallad again attacked on wounded Lukata in anger and killed her.

But Suggha's assassination pushed the whole Kaalaghat in a strange noise of silence. The assassination of Suggha drowned all the animals in the ocean of sadness. Bhaggu was also weeping when Bhallad saw him. Bhallad ordered wolves to kill Bhaggu.

"But you promised to forgive us if I support you. And I did everything whatever you instructed." said Bhaggu in fear.

"I promised you to leave your family alive, not you." said Bhallad and signaled wolves to kill him. After killing Bhaggu, wolves freed his family.

Then all the animals of the Kaalaghat gathered and accompanied Bhallad at the funeral of Suggha.

From that day, all the animals started roaming inside Kaalaghat and Rock-field freely, with no fear. After seven days of condolence, all the animals of Kaalaghat were celebrating the end of hyenas, but Bhallad was sitting alone close to the grave of Suggha; beside Kaalan's. Tears from his eyes were uncontrollably dribbling……

***** THE END*****

www.ingramcontent.com/pod-product-compliance
Lightning Source LLC
Chambersburg PA
CBHW071237140726
47996CB00007B/2638